# Peg.

# Titles in the Bunch:

Baby Bear Comes Home

Big Dog and Little Dog Visit the Moon

Clumsy Clumps and the Baby Moon

Delilah Digs for Treasure

Dilly and the Goody-Goody  Happy Sad

Horse in the House  I don't want to say Yes!

Juggling with Jeremy  Keeping Secrets

Mabel and Max  Magnificent Mummies

Midnight in Memphis  Millie's Party

Monster Eyeballs  Mouse Flute  The Nut Map

Owl in the House  Peg  Promise you won't be cross

Riff-Raff Rabbit  Rosie and the Robbers

Runaway Fred  Tom's Hats

First published in Great Britain 1999 by Mammoth
an imprint of Egmont Children's Books Limited.
239 Kensington High Street, London W8 6SA
Published in hardback by Heinemann Library,
a division of Reed Educational and Professional Publishing Limited
by arrangement with Egmont Children's Books Limited.
Text copyright © Maddie Stewart 1999
Illustrations copyright © Bee Willey 1999
The Author and Illustrator have asserted their moral rights.
Paperback ISBN 0 7497 3260 1
Hardback ISBN 0 434 80222 0
10 9 8 7 6 5 4 3 2 1
A CIP catalogue record for this title is available from the British Library.
Printed and bound in Dubai by Oriental Press Limited.

# Peg

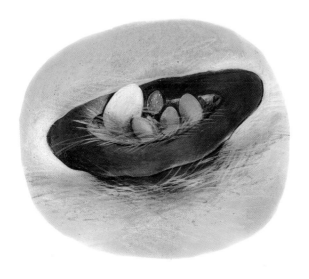

Maddie Stewart

Illustrated by Bee Willey

Blue Bananas

For the three
boys on the farm,
Hal, Max and James
M.S.


For Leopold.
Lots of love and XXX
B.W.

Farmer Henry had hundreds of hens.

He didn't want Peg

For she'd only one leg.

So he left her behind

For the fox to find.

Benjamin Bottomly found her instead.

He carried her home

To a little warm bed.

6

Benjamin tucked Peg under his arm,

And took her to see his father's farm.

Pig fed her piglets.

Horse played with her foal.

The cat and her kittens

Licked milk from a bowl.

The cow and her calf were taking a stroll.

Peg felt sad that she wasn't a mother,

With chicks all around

To need her and love her.

Benjamin gently put Peg on the ground.

She *hopped*

And she *flopped*

*oops!*

And she fell all around.

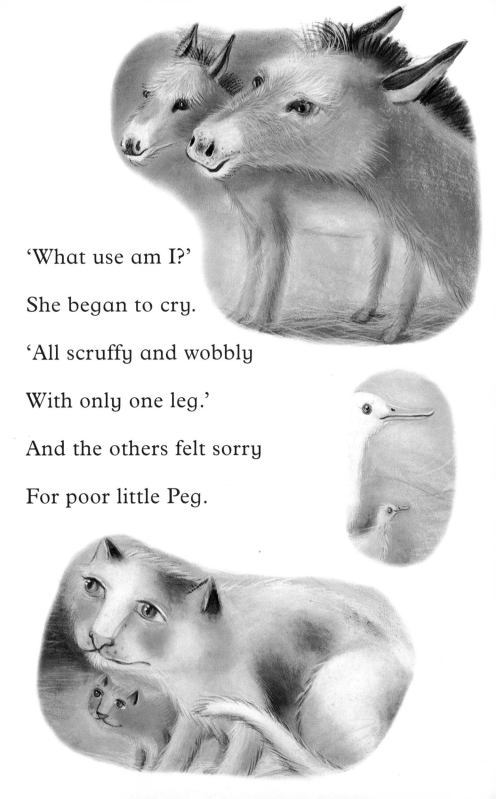

'What use am I?'

She began to cry.

'All scruffy and wobbly

With only one leg.'

And the others felt sorry

For poor little Peg.

Benjamin Bottomly said, 'Don't cry!

Soon you'll be singing a sweet lullaby.

You shall have a family, dear little Peg,

For you don't need a leg to sit on an egg.'

So Benjamin Bottomly

Asked here and there:

'Does anyone have any eggs to spare?'

What a lovely big egg.

18

'Here's one large egg

That's come from the zoo,

But does that scruff

Know what to do?'

'Know what to do?

Of course I do!

I'll sit on this egg

That comes from the zoo.

I'll keep it warm,

From dusk until dawn,

And when at last

My chick is born,

I'll give it my love

And I'll feed it my corn.'

22

The chick that hatched grew big and fat.

He looked quite cute in Benjamin's hat!

He loved his mother best of all.

He thought it nice that she was small.

Benjamin Bottomley asked here and there:

'Does anyone have any eggs to spare?'

'Know what to do?

Of course I do!

I'll sit on these eggs

All shiny and new.

26

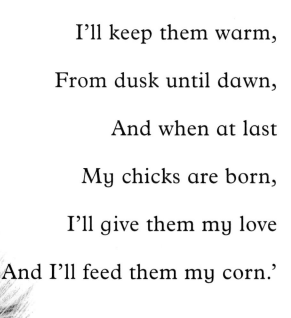

I'll keep them warm,

From dusk until dawn,

And when at last

My chicks are born,

I'll give them my love

And I'll feed them my corn.'


Two little chicks

Hatched out soon.

On a sunny day

In the month of June.

As they got bigger

Their feathers grew

In brilliant colours

Of gold, green and blue.

They spread their tails in the morning sun

As they preened and pranced

For their darling mum.

Benjamin Bottomley asked here and there:

'Does anyone else have eggs to spare?'

'I have a few, all speckled and blue.

But does that scruff know what to do?'

Soon Peg will have the biggest family on the farm.

'Know what to do?

Of course I do!

I'll sit on these eggs

All speckled and blue.

I'll keep them warm,

From dusk until dawn,

And when at last

My chicks are born,

I'll give them my love

And I'll feed them

My corn.'

Three eggs cracked

And chicks were hatched.

The chicks grew bigger every day.

And chose the pond as a place to play.

They followed their mum
When she went for a toddle.

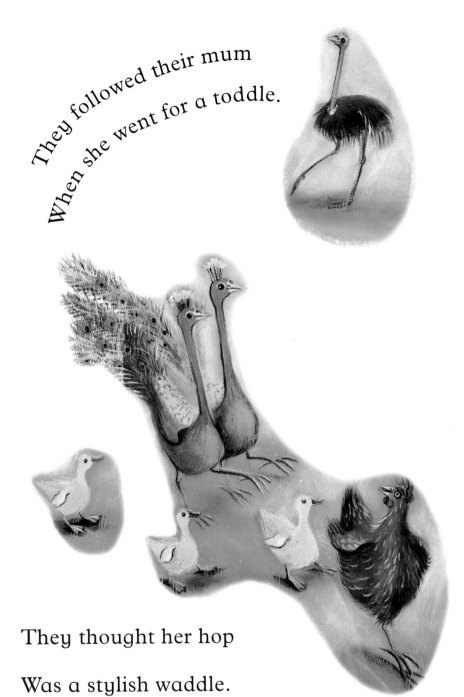

They thought her hop

Was a stylish waddle.

Still Benjamin Bottomly

Asked here and there:

'Does anyone have any eggs to spare?'

'I have four, I found on the floor.

But are you sure

You still want more?'

'Yes! I'm sure I still want more.

I want to mother chicks galore.

I'll sit on these eggs

You found on the floor.

I know how to do it,        One,

I've done it before!

I'll keep them warm,

From dusk until dawn,

And when at last my chicks are born,

I'll give them my love

And I'll feed them my corn.'   Two,

The eggs were hatched –

Three,

Four!

39

The chicks grew fast and learned to fly,

Up and away in the clear blue sky.

And as their mother hopped along,

They sang for her their sweetest song.

A beautiful hen,

All shiny and sleek,

Came into the farmyard

To take a peek.

43

'And who is that hen

So scruffy and lame,

So utterly useless

And horribly plain?'

44

45

That's our mother

And we love her!